BIGBear,
SMALL Mouse

Karma Wilson

Illustrations by
Jane Chapman

Margaret K. McElderry Books • New York London Toronto Sydney New Delhi

Mouse hops onto Bear.
He is careful not to fall.
Bear is big, big, **BIG!**
Mouse is small, small, **small!**

Small Mouse,
big Bear.

Bear and Mouse both wave
to their friends as they go past.

Badger moseys **slowly,**
but Hare runs very *fast!*

Slow Badger, **fast** Hare.
Small Mouse, **big** Bear!

What's that up above?
There's a flutter in the sky.

Wren is flying **low**,
while Owl is soaring **high**.

There's a clatter in the glen
High Owl, **low** Wren.
Slow Badger, **fast** Hare.
Small Mouse, **big** Bear!

Mole and Gopher tunnel up
and join the happy crowd.

The sun sets on the **quiet** woods, but all the friends are **loud!**

Quiet woods, **loud** friends.
High Owl, **low** Wren.
Slow Badger, **fast** Hare.
Small Mouse, **big** Bear!

Raven flies down from the sky.
"Look, here comes a storm!"

Outside it's getting wet and **cold**,

but the lair is nice and **warm!**

All together, gathered there.
Cold night, **warm** lair.
Quiet woods, **loud** friends.
High Owl, **low** Wren.
Slow Badger, **fast** Hare.
Small Mouse . . .

To Rita and Rachel,
two librarians putting big ideas
in the minds of little people!
Thank you for your support of children's literacy.
—K. W.

For Jonah
—J. C.

THE BEAR BOOKS • MARGARET K. MCELDERRY BOOKS • An imprint of Simon & Schuster Children's Publishing Division • 1230 Avenue of the Americas, New York, New York 10020 • Text copyright © 2016 by Karma Wilson • Illustrations copyright © 2016 by Jane Chapman • All rights reserved, including the right of reproduction in whole or in part in any form. • MARGARET K. MCELDERRY BOOKS is a trademark of Simon & Schuster, Inc. • For information about special discounts for bulk purchases, please contact Simon & Schuster Special Sales at 1-866-506-1949 or business@simonandschuster.com. • The Simon & Schuster Speakers Bureau can bring authors to your live event. For more information or to book an event, contact the Simon & Schuster Speakers Bureau at 1-866-248-3049 or visit our website at www.simonspeakers.com. • Book design by Lauren Rille • The text for this book was set in Adobe Caslon. • The illustrations for this book were rendered in acrylic paint. • Manufactured in China • 0916 SCP • First edition • 10 9 8 7 6 5 4 3 2 1 • Library of Congress Cataloging-in-Publication Data • Names: Wilson, Karma, author. | Chapman, Jane, illustrator. • Title: Big bear, small mouse / Karma Wilson ; illustrated by Jane Chapman. • Description: 1st edition. | New York : Margaret K. McElderry Books, 2016. • Summary: "A big bear and a small mouse discover all of the opposites between their animal friends"—Provided by publisher. • Identifiers: LCCN 2015044616 | ISBN 978-1-4814-5971-6 (hardcover) | ISBN 978-1-4814-5972-3 (eBook) • Subjects: CYAC: Stories in rhyme. | English language—Synonyms and antonyms—Fiction. | Bears—Fiction. | Mice—Fiction. | Animals—Fiction. | BISAC: JUVENILE FICTION / Concepts / Opposites. | JUVENILE FICTION / Animals / General. | JUVENILE FICTION / Social Issues / Friendship. • Classification: LCC PZ8.3.W6976 Bi 2016 | DDC [E]—dc23 LC record available at https://lccn.loc.gov/2015044616